This book belongs to:

**For our children and their ideas for this book
and to all the Jack and Boo fans!**

Special thanks to Dinosaur Isle for their expert help!

Also available:
Jack and Boo's Bucket of Treasures
Jack and Boo's Wild Wood
Jack and Boo's Snowy Day

First published in Great Britain by Beachy Books in 2013

For more information visit
www.beachybooks.com

ISBN: 978-0-9562980-3-4

Jack and Boo's DINOSAUR ISLAND

Dinosaur Island

Alum Bay
Compton Brook
Hanover Point
Brighstone Bay
Shepherd's Chine
Chale Bay
Whale Chine
Sandown Bay
Yaverland
Whitecliff Bay

Written by Philip Bell   Illustrated by Eleanor Bell

Beachy Books

www.beachybooks.com

On Dinosaur Island gulls on groynes brace
against the last puff of a storm, which blows
frothy waves onto flat bronze sand.

Jack and I play on Sandown Bay digging
a giant nest for a giant dinosaur
to lay her giant eggs.

'Hold the sea back, Jack!'

dinosaur eggs

Jack stares at the ships on
the horizon. 'It's endless!'

'The mummy Iguanodon is coming!' I shout.

Jack runs along the shore. 'Let's look for fossils!'

Exploring the ancient sands of Yaverland
looking for fossils, once wrapped
in coloured cliffs, preserved
for millions of years, unwrapped
by eager storms, sorted by tides,
hidden on the shore.

Otodus
'shark tooth'

Jack has eagle eyes and picks up fossilised
wood, glinting with fool's gold, and a shark
tooth. I find a heavy ball of natural iron like a
rusty pearl and coprolite—dino poo!

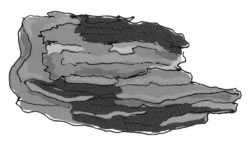

fossil wood

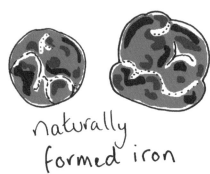

naturally
formed iron

coprolite—
dinosaur poo

Rabbits scamper, as fast as Eotyrannus,
into burrows when we run down
to Whitecliff Bay for a play
on the beach.

Then we explore under
gleaming chalk made
from a sea of dead creatures
(too small to see).

echinoid
'sea urchin'

We little urchins clamber over boulders
as big as dinosaur jaws and fossilised
sea urchins and maybe
a belemnite
or two.

belemnite

We have a whale of a time walking along
Whale Chine where, years ago, a whale
beached down on Chale.

'It's sooo high up!' I say.

'Be careful, Boo! Hold my hand!'

Iguanodon
skeleton

We stroll along the dinosaur footpath, long
grass bending in the breeze, where herds of
Iguanodon marched on their migration,
Valdosaurus grazed and Istiodactylus flocked.

The cliff has fallen away in places, after rain
and wind, to reveal Iguanodon bones as pink
as their rocky graves.

Carrying a picnic, we race along the dusty footpath like hunted Hypsilophodon following the trickling river from a gap in the soft rock and zigzagging along Shepherd's Chine until the water merges with the twinkling sea.

bone fragment

Scrambling up shingle shelves on an empty Brighstone Bay carrying buckets of treasures and a fossil bone of a meat-toothed three-clawed hunter called Neovenator, which died in a flood covered in mud a long time ago.

Clanking down steps to Compton Bay
for a run on the shore,
which curls like a dinosaur's tail,
in search of ammonites,
slipped from the land
onto sand.

ammonite

Surfers balance on
rolling waves as the shadow
of a paraglider passes
high above our heads,
wings spread like pterosaurs,
the flying reptiles of the sky, circling on the
warm air and spying on walkers, the size of
ants, marching towards Tennyson Down.

The cliffs are so red against the blue sky where we love to pick up the interesting stones in the hope they might be a funny-named fossil of an old dead sea creature.

I climb onto rusty red rock and pretend
I've got big stomping dinosaur feet.

'Jack, look at me! I'm as tall as a Pelorosaurus!'

Jack laughs. 'They were taller than the cliffs!'

bivalve

crinoid

brachiopod

Walking over fossil logs to the smooth sand
of Brook Bay, we look for rocks filled with
tiny fossilised sea snail shells,
shaped like ice cream cones,
and scales of turtle shells
and delicate stars.

turtle shell

We see three stone claws in the sand made
by a dinosaur, which once roamed on
hind legs, so heavy it sank into mud
and left footprints on the beach.

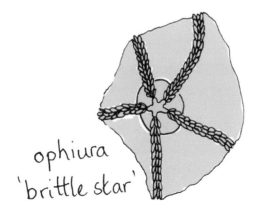

ophiura
'brittle star'

Turritella
gastropod

On a falling tide, we make our way around to Hanover Point, stepping over mudstones, soaked with slippery seaweed, and fossilised tree trunks, revealed by retreating waves.

Jack points. 'Boo, look! A dinosaur foot!'

'How was it made?' I say.

'Dinosaur footprints filled with mud like a giant jelly mould,' Jack explains.
'Over millions of years they turned to stone and left these fossilised footcasts!'

I spot another. 'Let's search for them all!'

We soar above the rainbow-striped cliffs of Alum Bay as high as a pterosaur over white stacks in the sea, which are sharper than the armoured spikes of a Polacanthus.

'Jack, did you see something in the water?'

'Is it a mermaid, Boo? Is it a sea serpent?'

'No,' I say, 'it's a fishysaur!'

As the sun sets on The Needles, we ride home with our few precious fossils and dream that one day we might discover a new dinosaur buried on Dinosaur Island.

DINOSAUR SPOTTER

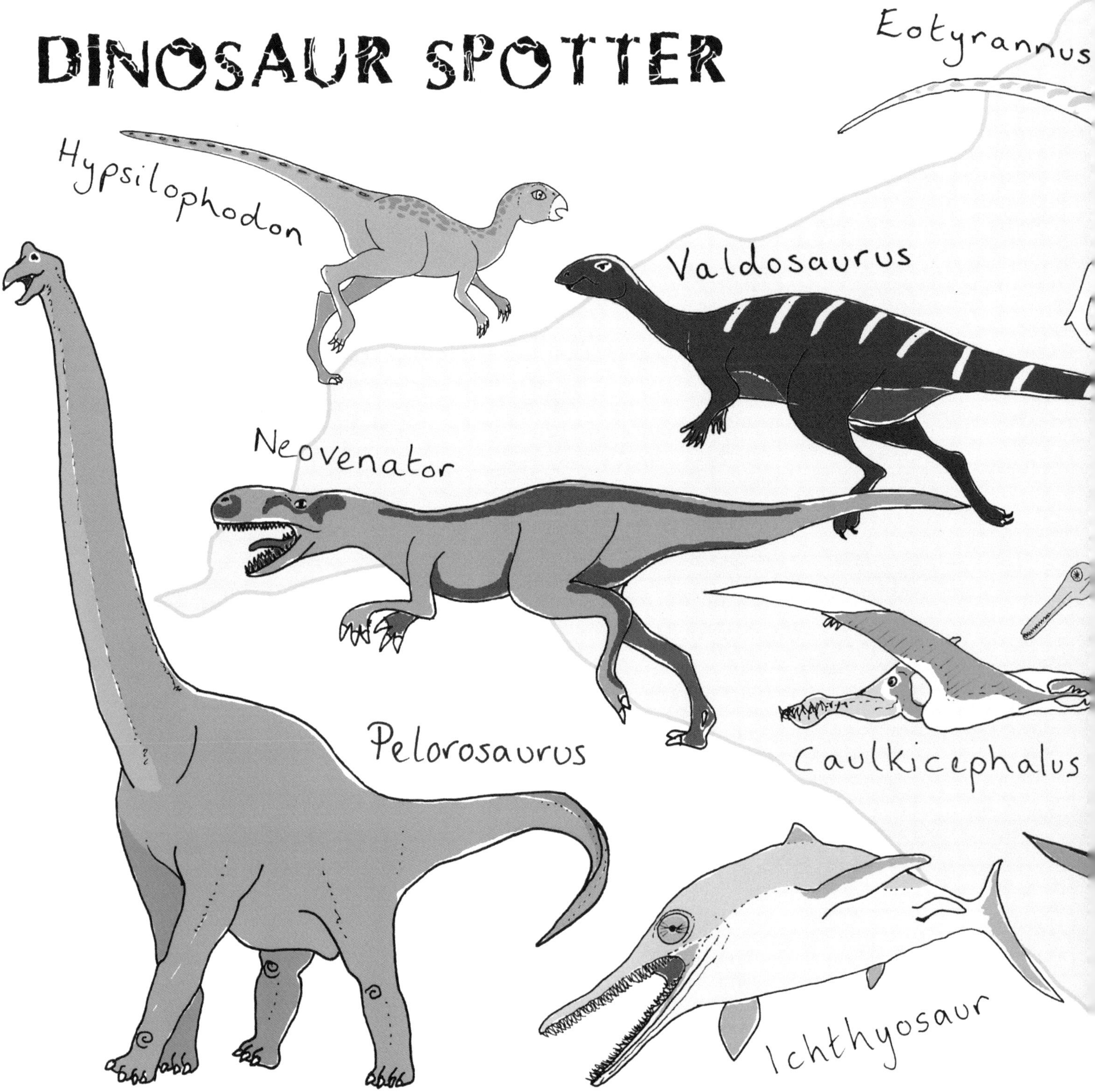

Eotyrannus

Hypsilophodon

Valdosaurus

Neovenator

Pelorosaurus

Caulkicephalus

Ichthyosaur

Baryonyx

Iguanodon

Istiodactylus

Polacanthus

pterosaurs

Ornithocheirus

Leptocleidus

Vectidraco
daisymorrisae

FOSSIL SPOTTER

belemnite

Ostrea
vectensis
'Wight
Oyster'

cut away of animal
body when alive

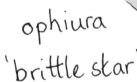

bone
fragment

turtle shell

ophiura
'brittle star'

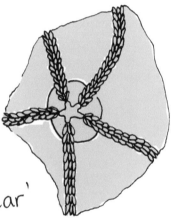

dinosaur
eggs

crinoid

brachiopod

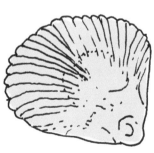

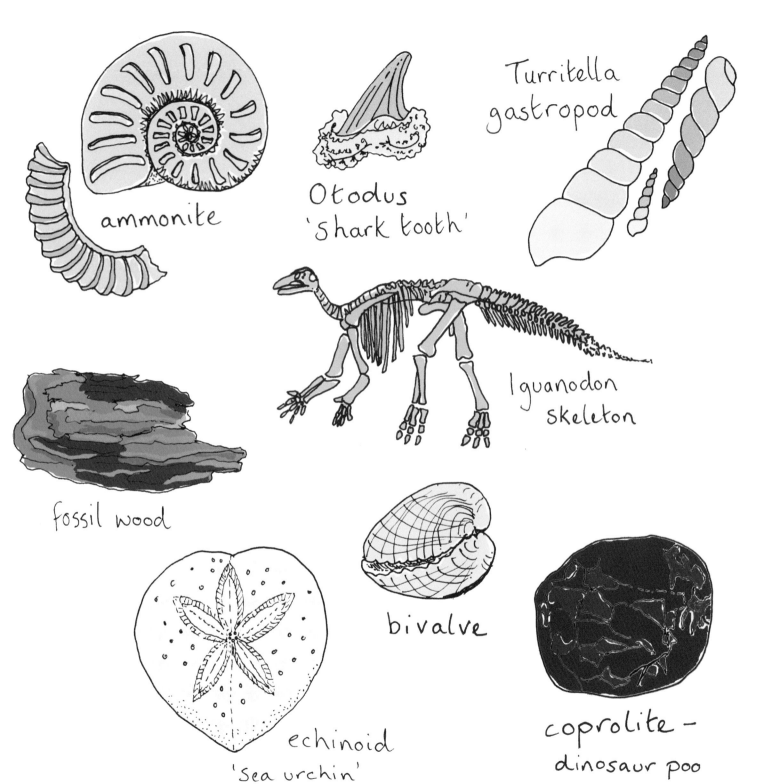

ammonite

Otodus
'shark tooth'

Turritella
gastropod

fossil wood

Iguanodon
skeleton

echinoid
'sea urchin'

bivalve

coprolite –
dinosaur poo